CW00847111

Written by
FRANCES VELODY * Illustrated by
MARK BEECH

ALBUS BOOKS

First published in Great Britain in 2021 by Albus Books

A CIP catalogue record for this book is available from the British Library
ISBN: 978-1-8384120-0-5

Book design by Mandy Norman

Printed and bound in Great Britain by Biddles Books, Castle House,
East Winch Road, Blackborough End, King's Lynn, Norfolk PE32 1SF

For Ana and Alex

THE CHARACTERS

MONSIEUR ALPHONSE
The Famous Chef

He has two deputy chefs (sous-chefs) to help him.

Monsieur Gaston and Madame Sylvie have
a couple of assistant chefs (commis chefs) to help them.

Here are the guests who are coming to eat the wonderful food in Monsieur Alphonse's famous restaurar

MADAME LEGRAND

Her name means 'Mrs Large', which is appropriate.

MONSIEUR LEGRAND

His name means 'Mr Large', which doesn't fit him nearly as well as his wife.

MADEMOISELLE PAPILLON

Her name means 'Miss Butterfly', which she thinks is a very pretty name. It suits her because she likes pretty things.

DR PERROQUET

His name means 'Dr Parrot'. He doesn't like it as much as Mademoiselle Papillon likes hers.

PROFESSEURE POISSON ROUGE

Her name means 'Professor Goldfish'. In her work she studies sea-creatures – especially oysters.

MONSIEUR POISSON ROUGE

He is the husband of the professor. He likes oysters as well.

MONSIEUR ET MADAME CANARD

Their names mean 'Mr and Mrs Duck'. Do you think it suits them?

The story begins . . .

In the heart of the French countryside is a château.* It is small and square with four circular towers, one at each corner. In the sun it shines rose pink and the light glistens on the towers' turrets.

It sits on the top of a hill with a grand view over the countryside and overlooks La Lune, the narrow river far below.

*A château is a historic country house in France.

Once upon a time a famous Duke lived here but now it is the home of a restaurant called *Le Chien d'or.*★ People come from far and wide and leave promising to return.

In the kitchen you will find Monsieur Alphonse, the Chef de Cuisine.★

It is Monsieur Alphonse who every day ties his ears up, puts his toque* on his head and his chef's whites and begins to weave his culinary magic.

He is assisted by his two sous-chefs, Madame Sylvie and Monsieur Gaston, who in turn supervise the small team of commis chefs responsible for meat, vegetables, pastry and sauces.

*A toque is the tall white hat chefs wear.

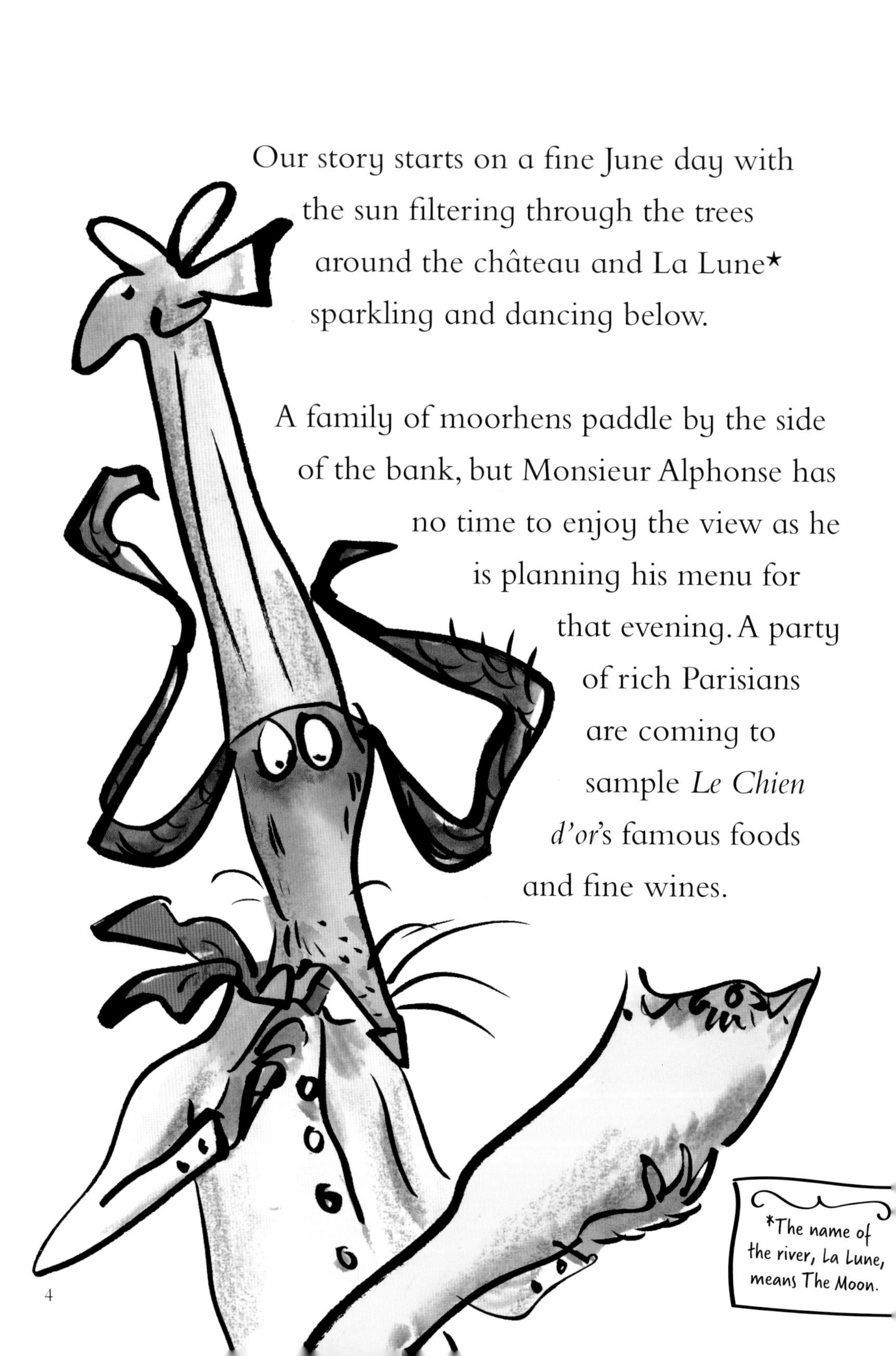

Our story starts on a fine June day with the sun filtering through the trees around the château and La Lune* sparkling and dancing below.

A family of moorhens paddle by the side of the bank, but Monsieur Alphonse has no time to enjoy the view as he is planning his menu for that evening. A party of rich Parisians are coming to sample *Le Chien d'or*'s famous foods and fine wines.

*The name of the river, La Lune, means The Moon.

Monsieur Alphonse writes in his beautiful pawscript:

There is only one menu as Monsieur Alphonse knows what he wants people to eat.

He says to Sylvie and Gaston, 'The boudin blanc will be the **BIGGEST** sausage these Parisians have ever seen. I will impress them not only with its splendid taste but also with its **SHEER SIZE!**'

Sylvie and Gaston are already impressed. They find Monsieur Alphonse and his great gastronomic gestures inspiring. He favours size and scale, each dish designed to delight and thrill his guests.

All day long the kitchen prepares. Sylvie hops on her bicycle and cycles to the market. At the boucherie* she implores the butcher to make the **BIGGEST SAUSAGE** France has ever seen.

'It must be the size of an **elephant's trunk** and **TWICE THE WIDTH!**'

The butcher smiles and winks; he is used to Monsieur Alphonse's requests.

*A boucherie is a butcher's shop.

While the butcher prepares the sausage, Sylvie beetles around the market, **smelling** and **SQUEEZING** produce until she is satisfied she has only the best.

While she is out, Gaston and his assistants prepare the tables with the restaurant's solid silver cutlery, white linen tablecloths and crystal wine glasses.

And Monsieur Alphonse? He lies down in his hammock which is suspended between two pear trees, puts his ears over his eyes and has a little dog nap. He must preserve his strength for the preparation of the feast.

At five o'clock a small passenger boat, *Le Toutou*,★ arrives from Aboieville,★ a mile upstream, where the train connects to Paris. Monsieur Alphonse hears its engines, flicks away an ear and opens one eye.

He knows it will take the passengers half an hour to climb up through the château's gardens from La Lune, or twenty minutes if they use the tiny funicular railway to pull them up the hill.

★*Le Toutou* means *The Doggie*, and Aboieville means Bark Town. You can understand why Monsieur Alphonse feels at home here.

The carriage of the railway is called *Le Chat noir*,* a name which Monsieur Alphonse is not at all happy about. When he hears the grinding of the railway's wheels, he is always forced to run into the kitchen and stir his sauces in an agitated manner!

*Le Chat noir means The Black Cat – now you know why Monsieur Alphonse doesn't like it!

Sylvie and Gaston have done much preparation and now is the time for Monsieur Alphonse to take the stage.

He takes a pinch of this and a sprinkle of that and waves a furry, but very clean, paw over his saucepans.

He adds a little brandy, rubs his claws together;

there is a **SPARK**,

A BANG

and flames which turn

BLUE, **PURPLE** and **GOLD**.

Monsieur Alphonse is very energetic;

he **leaps**,

he **twirls**,

he **dances**.

He hastily
re-curls a whisker
where the flames have
singed it and **leaps** again.

It is time for the last-minute preparations.

he tastes again
and then he smiles.

PERFECTION!

Monsieur Alphonse cocks an ear as he hears the guests arriving and rolls his eyes as he hears the haughty tones of one of the ladies. This is Madame Legrand, and he has been told she is very bossy.

‘Where is my room?’ she says. ‘I want to inspect my bath to make sure it is big enough!’

Not only does Madame Legrand inspect her bath, she examines everything.

She looks at the
gardens to check the
roses are fragrant.

She runs her fingers over the
chandelier in the dining room
to check it has been dusted.

She even sticks her
sharp nose into the
kitchen to see what
they are having
for dinner.

Monsieur Alphonse is
not impressed with
that at all!

Madame Legrand is quite tired after all this activity and goes upstairs to lie down. But first she says to her husband, 'Look after my pearls. I want to wear them at dinner tonight; I want to impress!'

'Yes, dear,' says Monsieur Legrand. He is small, tired and rather fed up.

Madame Legrand hands over the pearls to her husband. She is very proud of them and they certainly do not go unnoticed by the other guests, who stare at them enviously. Monsieur Alphonse, who has been trying to keep a low profile as he lurks behind a large aspidistra, notices their reactions and his eyes narrow.

He has put all his energies into creating a marvellous feast and he hopes that his guests won't have their minds distracted by other beautiful creations. . .

The diners are due to gather for dinner at eight o'clock and preparations whirl in the kitchen so everything will be ready on time.

The first course is served and proclaimed a

You may not think so, but snails are a real delicacy in France and Monsieur Alphonse's creation with garlic butter and a splash of cognac is superb.

But then there is a wail. Madame Legrand shrieks,

'WHERE ARE **MY PEARLS?**

THEY ARE **NOT** AROUND MY NECK!

SOMEONE HAS **STOLEN** THEM!

CALL **THE POLICE.**

DON'T LET ANYONE **LEAVE!**'

The other guests look bemused, Monsieur Legrand puts his head in his hands and, unnoticed, Monsieur Alphonse, who was hovering by the kitchen door, slips away.

He goes into his big food larder where hams hang from the ceiling, cheeses rest in waxed paper and garlic is tied in big bunches. He disappears behind a huge box of fresh peaches.

Anyone passing by outside the larder may have heard rustling, scraping and other interesting noises . . . but no one is near.

The door of the larder springs open and into the dining room strides a figure in a green suit, deerstalker and tweed cape. The guests, by turn, look stunned, amazed or shocked. Madame Legrand gasps.

'I AM INSPECTOR HOUND,' says the figure, tucking an escaping ear back into his deerstalker, 'and I am here to solve this crime!'

He then turns to Sylvie and Gaston and adds in an undertone, '. . . You may wish to turn the heat down under the sausage to prevent it drying up.'

Inspector Hound strides around the dining room. He is an impressive figure and the guests gaze at him with wide eyes.

'I will interview each of you in my study . . . but very quickly, as the boudin blanc – that enormous sausage – must not suffer!'

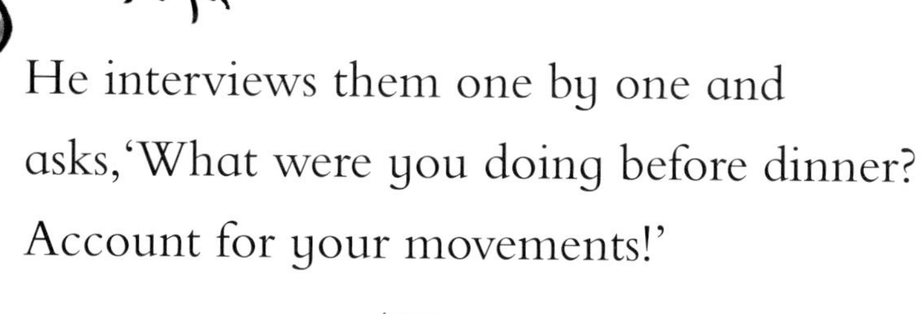

He interviews them one by one and asks, 'What were you doing before dinner? Account for your movements!'

MADEMOISELLE MARIE PAPILLON

She was fluttering in her room, getting ready for dinner.

MADAME MONIQUE CANARD

She was in the library, reading a book about lakes.

MONSIEUR PIERRE CANARD

He was waddling in the rose garden.

DR JEAN PERROQUET

He was having a quick nap before dinner (with his head under his arm).

PROFESSEURE ADÈLE POISSON ROUGE

She was strolling around the fish-pond.

MONSIEUR MICHEL POISSON ROUGE

He was wallowing in his bath.

Inspector Hound strides back into the dining room, sits at the table and rests his chin on his paws. He looks carefully at each of the guests in turn before focusing on Professeure and Monsieur Poisson Rouge and narrowing his eyes.

Professeure Poisson Rouge looks angry. 'Why are you looking at me? I had nothing to do with this. I think you should put your shiny nose into the business of Monsieur and Madame Canard. They needed the money!'

The Canards jump to their feet. 'How dare you!' exclaims Monsieur Canard. 'Surely Mademoiselle Papillon is the one to talk to. She loves beautiful jewellery and some of it has been acquired in rather unusual circumstances. She would find Madame Legrand's pearls impossible to resist!'

Mademoiselle Papillon bursts into tears. 'Yes, I love beautiful things, but I would never steal. Perhaps the Inspector should look at Dr Perroquet. He has never been friends with Madame Legrand – ever since she built her great big house right next to his little cottage.'

Dr Perroquet rolls his eyes and looks bored. 'That is old news. Let's go back to the Poissons Rouges. They had plenty of time to steal the pearls and hide them, perhaps near the fish-pond? And the motive? Professeure Poisson Rouge's research into oysters. She doesn't approve of taking pearls from "poor oysters".'

And then they are all jumping to their feet and **SHOUTING** at each other. Professeure Poisson Rouge pokes Dr Perroquet in the stomach with a spoon, Madame Canard kicks her chair leg and Monsieur Poisson Rouge hits the table with his fist, putting his hand straight into the butter.

Finally, Mademoiselle Papillon throws a bread roll at Monsieur Canard which hits him right on the nose.

Inspector Hound suddenly **BANGS** the dinner gong and everybody freezes! They all stand perfectly still, apart from Monsieur Poisson Rouge, who is wiping butter from his hand, and Monsieur Canard, who is wrapping his serviette round his swollen nose.

Inspector Hound stands up, his nose **twitching**. It twitches right over to Madame Legrand and has a good sniff. Madame Legrand looks quite startled and then quite frightened as his nostrils flare around her large fingers. Inspector Hound removes a crumb of something from underneath one of her many rings and puts it carefully in his handkerchief. Exhibit A!

Inspector Hound claps his paws together and smiles. He moves to the head of the table and turns to address the guests.

'MESDAMES! MESSIEURS!*
I have solved this case . . . Bring me the ENORMOUS sausage!'

Sylvie returns with the boudin blanc, beautifully presented on a bed of lentils and garnished with lemon and parsley. She places it on the table.

Inspector Hound looks at the sausage – a long, lingering look. Then he stares at his guests one by one.

Finally, his eyes settle upon Madame Legrand. 'Madame, you went into the kitchen when you arrived.'

'But of course,' says Madame Legrand. 'I couldn't wait to know what we were having for dinner!'

'But I put it to you, Madame,' says Inspector Hound, 'that later, after you had dressed for dinner, you sneaked **BACK** into the kitchen a second time, to marvel at the creation of this exquisite dish.'

'But of course,' says Madame Legrand. 'I like to see the preparation of everything I am going to eat! I am a well-known gourmet!'*

*A gourmet is a person who adores fine food – and knows a lot about it.

Inspector Hound picks up a knife and pierces the sausage. Once more he addresses the guests:

'Madame Legrand was leaning over the sausage when it was stuffed with extra garlic and a soupçon* of chilli and before it was, if I may say, expertly stitched up with this thread of chives.'

He pulls out the thread of chives and dangles it before the guests.

'Her pearls came loose and fell into this remarkable creation! My excellent sense of smell led me to detect sausage-meat on her fingers – when she had a quick taste, a piece of it became lodged under one of her beautiful rings.'

With a flick of his knife the sausage is open and

They have come loose from their thread and roll one by one onto the platter, each pearl now delicately scented with garlic and spices.

Madame Legrand claps her hands together.

'YOU ARE A MARVEL, INSPECTOR HOUND!'

The other guests also applaud and, having removed the pearls, Sylvie expertly sews up the sausage and slices it for the guests.

IT IS PERFECTION!

'What an amazing investigation! You did it so quickly!' exclaims Monsieur Canard, but Inspector Hound has already slipped away. The guests are confused.

'WHERE IS HE?'

'WHERE DID THE GREAT DETECTIVE GO?'

Monsieur Alphonse watches with pleasure the consumption of the enormous sausage from the kitchen window. He puts the final touches to the îles flottantes.

The guests cannot stop talking about the exciting revelations of the evening, having first apologised to each other for their very bad behaviour. They speak of the fantastic meal and the lost pearls but most of all they wonder at the brilliant and mysterious detective who solved the case with such elegance and charm.

But Sylvie and Gaston, quietly serving the dessert and pouring the fine wines, smile and say nothing.

AND NOW . . .

To celebrate Inspector Hound's successful resolution of this culinary conundrum, Monsieur Alphonse has created a new recipe for you to try at home. Don't forget to ask for some adult help!

YOUR RECIPE

My boudin blanc is so **enormous** that it's not possible to make it at home. So I have created another sausage recipe specially for you and your family to try. I hope you will like it!

It's a sausage and lentil 'Hérisson' (that means 'hedgehog' – yes, it really does look like a hedgehog!). This recipe will teach you how to create six of these beautiful and tasty little creatures. You can also make a vegetarian version.

- ★ One sheet of ready-rolled puff pastry (approximately 350mm x 230mm)
- ★ Six high-meat pork chipolatas (chipolatas are a type of small sausage)
- ★ One 440g tin (drained) or 250g ready-cooked puy lentils
- ★ One egg (or 4 eggs if you are making the vegetarian version)
- ★ 18 whole cloves

AND THIS IS THE EQUIPMENT YOU WILL NEED:

- ★ A large baking tray
- ★ Greaseproof paper
- ! A sharp knife (be very careful!)
- ! Scissors (careful with these too!)
- ★ A tablespoon
- ★ A pastry brush
- ★ A saucepan to boil 3 eggs (if making the vegetarian version)

Turn the oven on, so that it starts heating up, ready for you to bake your hedgehogs.

★ 220°C (or 200°C if you have a fan oven).

★ If your oven is gas, it's gas mark 6.

Use the scissors to cut the greaseproof paper to the right size to **line** your baking tray.

Now you need to use the knife to cut the pastry. Lay the sheet of pastry out **flat**, and cut it into **six rectangles**.

Put the lentils in a bowl and season them (this means stir in a little salt and pepper). Then place a heaped tablespoonful of the lentil mix **onto** each rectangle.

5 **Now comes the sausage!** You need one little chipolata sausage for each hedgehog. **Fold the sausage in half**, and gently pinch the two ends together to make a teardrop shape.

With your scissors, make little snips in the curved edge to stop your sausage straightening out.

Now put the sausage on the lentil pile.
★ For the vegetarian version, place half a hard-boiled egg on the lentil pile, instead of the sausage.

6 Now it's time to start making it look like a **hedgehog**. First, you need to crack the egg into a bowl and beat it with a fork until the yellow and white are mixed together.

The next step is to **fold over two corners** of the pastry so they overlap to make a **pointed end** – this will be the hedgehog's nose. Use the pastry brush to paint on some egg to help the pastry corners stick together.

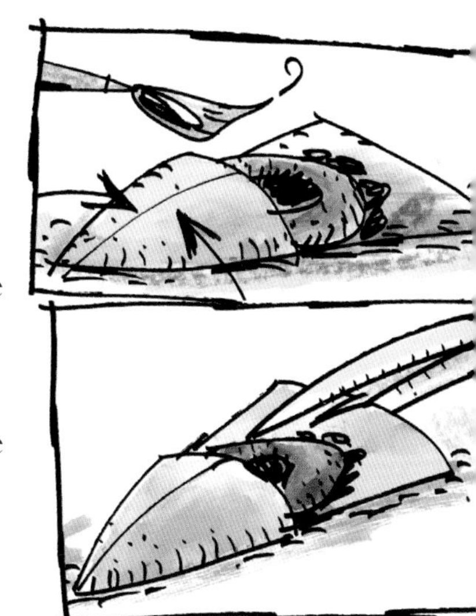

7 Use the scissors to snip the edges of the rest of the pastry to **make flaps**.

8 Brush the flaps with egg, and then bring them up and stick them together. This will make the hedgehog's tummy.

Don't worry if your hedgehog is looking a bit messy now. Turn it over and gently pat it into a hedgehog-like shape. Paint it all over with egg. This will help it turn a lovely brown colour in the oven.

10 Now we're going to give it a face: poke in three of the cloves to be its eyes and nose. Then take the scissors and snip V-shaped notches all over its body. While it cooks in the oven, these V-shaped notches will puff up to become the hedgehog's spines.

11 And now it's time to put your hedgehogs on the baking tray and into the oven! Ask your adult helper to do this for you, as the oven will be very hot by now. Leave the hedgehogs in the oven for about 20 minutes, until they are golden brown.

12 When they come out of the oven, let them cool down a bit and remove the cloves before you eat them – and then,

Frances Velody

Frances sharing precious moments with Alexander (3), Anastasia (7) and William (10)

My wife Frances was always smiling. Her huge joy in life and happiness when surrounded by family and friends was matched by her passion for her career in education and outreach in the world of heritage and her longstanding ambition to write stories for children. So Inspector Hound was born, inspired by the tales she would read to our children, Anastasia and Alexander, and her nephew, William.

Unfortunately, time was not on Frances's side, and her death in her forties meant that these stories have never been published – until now, through the hard work of her beloved sister Alison and the overwhelming generosity of all those who loved Frances. We thank them all, with particular mention of her aunt, Lesley Goulden, for all her support, and her friend, chef Gileng Salter, for the recipe.

Frances discovered Mark Beech before she died and was absolutely delighted with his characterisation of Inspector Hound. Years later we are very grateful to Mark for picking up and finishing her project with such enthusiasm and care and for introducing us to the wonderful designer Mandy Norman.

We loved Frances and now we love that Inspector Hound has life, an active memorial for the kids so that Frances will not be time-locked in history, left behind just because her own clock stopped.

Nicholas Velody